NINE

Jo Ann Zueckert

Cover Design: Keryl Pesce

Published by Little Pink Press, P.O. Box 847, Beacon, NY 12508

ISBN-13: 978-1-7329494-4-7

Dedication

This book is dedicated to my three daughters, Kim, Karen, and Keryl, and to all those, who, despite their age, maintain the belief in magic, mystery, and love.

Preface

Sometimes unknowingly, we look for magic in our everyday lives. We all have a certain undefinable thing that is there, but most of us will not look beyond reality to find it. If we would all take a certain number or word, we might find that our entire lives revolve around that particular item.

Jo Ann Zueckert

Nine is a fascinating number. Most of our lives begin with 9, since the average pregnancy takes nine months. There are nine digits in our social security number. In Greek mythology, there are the nine Muses, the goddesses of song and poetry, the arts and science. Gypsy fortune tellers, when reading cards, believe that when a 9 is turned up, it is a sign of happiness. It is said that cats have nine lives. There are also nine planets in our solar system. The all time American favorite baseball teams have nine players. In the ninth grade of school, most of us choose our lifelong vocations.

In mathematics, the number 9 could almost be considered magical. Once one learns what two numbers, when added together make 9, the multiplication and division are simple. When adding any other number to 9, it is also very easy.

When multiplying any other number by 9, the result is one less than the number multiplied by 9, plus any other number added to it to make 9. For example: 9 x 4. First, write down 3 which is one less than 4. Then add 6 to it. Thus 9 x 4 = 36. Since we know that 3 plus 6 equals 9, the answer must be correct. In division, if the two numbers of the dividend equal 9, and it is to be divided by 9, the opposite holds true. When adding 9 to any other number, the answer is one less than that number, plus ten. In the subtraction, all one has to do is add the two numbers. If the problem were 17-9, you just add 1 plus 7, and the answer is 8.

Since most children fear the "nines," with these few little tricks, they might learn to love them. Try this simplified form. You will be amazed at how fast they can learn.

This book is entitled "9." It is a mystical, magical story, completely centered on the number 9.

Chapter 1

June, 1971

There in the master bedroom sat Madame Couquet. She was a beautiful woman for her age. She was kind and generous. You could see that radiating from her eyes. As she sat petting her cat, she thought of the past and began speaking to him as if he could understand her.

"I am thinking of my nephews, John and Louis, and of greedy little Michele. For years they have come to see me on my birthday and put on such airs. They have come with only the hope of getting a large inheritance. If only they knew what love is really like."

Her cat, who was curled up in her lap, looked up at her as if he could, in fact, understand.

"For many long years, I have observed them. How I did try to show them love."

"Dear, dear, Louis. What a handsome boy he always was. He had a way of flashing a smile that could get around anyone. That grin of his got him out of a lot of trouble, even when he was just a little tyke. I remember once when I had two goldfish, he reached into the bowl and squeezed them until they were dead. When I tried to reprimand him, his mother stepped in and said, "How can you get mad at anyone as cute as that?""

"He surely was a mischief maker. He had a pet way of doing things and blaming them on his little brother John. When Michele was just a baby, he'd bite her fingers, then run and tell his mother that John bit the baby. Now, Louis is getting some of his own medicine with that gold-digging wife of his. She nags him all the time about money. Heaven knows, they certainly are well enough off not to worry. Christina will be quite surprised to find out about their fortune!

Then there's John. He reminds me of a clumsy goose. Every time he tries to impress someone, he falls all over himself. When he was very young, he began to stutter. I did try hard to make him realize he was just as good as his brother and sister. Every time he stayed with me for a week, he began to show some improvement. The next time my brother brought him to me, he had slipped back to his old ways again. I really think the problem got worse when his mother ran off with that big movie producer to become a star. I wonder what ever became of her.

I can say this for him though; he always did show appreciation for even the smallest of things. Of course, he did have his awkward ways of trying to weasel things out of people. So I guess when he did receive anything, he had expected it anyway. Maybe if he knew about his inheritance, he'd lose some of that awkwardness."

As Madame Couquet rubbed her cat's neck, she smiled and laughed to herself a bit.

"Ah! Michele, I remember even when she was a child. Whenever I gave her three cookies and said, "One for Louis, one for John, and one for you," she'd run out and eat them all! Every time I traveled and brought them gifts, she wanted her own and theirs too.

Yes, she was her mother and father's darling. I guess they made her that way by giving her every-thing she always wanted. I can recall as if it were yesterday, the time John found a pretty white stone on the driveway. Michele saw it and cried and cried until they made him give it to her. She held it for about two minutes and threw it into the bushes. John tried to find it again, but to no avail.

Well, that's the way they were. After my brother died, they came to live with me. I tried to shape them into something better but it was just too late. They were already in their teens, and the molds were too strong to reform.

Yes, they will all be very much surprised. The town will have quite a shock. Maybe they too, will believe the rumors that I am a witch! A famous man once said, "The world will little note, nor long remember what is said here, but they will all remember what was done here."

You run along now. I am very tired. My work is finished in this world. Now I will go with a feeling of gratification."

Last week, she had celebrated her 81st birthday. She was not at all pleased with her relatives at the party. John had tried desperately to impress her, and all he accomplished was complete havoc. He did a great job of bumping into things and spilling food and drinks. His mastery was to trip all over himself.

Louis stopped whispering to Christina every time she walked near them. They seemed to have a private little game going between the two of them.

Whenever she looked at Michele, she could see her selfishness shining through that thick makeup, like a bright star in the heavens above.

Alas! They would certainly be surprised!

Chapter 2

Here it was. Three weeks after the funeral. In the enormous living room, they all stood around waiting for the lawyer to come and read the will. Michele started the conversation, "Well, it finally happened. After all those years, faithfully coming to her famous birthday parties, I hope she realized how much we cared about her. What do you think the old witch left to us?"

"Now Michele," said Louis, "you'd better hope the old lady didn't see through us. After all, she did have some uncanny ways about her."

"Th-Th-That's right," stuttered John. "W-W-We sh-sh-should have been a l-l-little nicer t-t-to her."

"If you can't talk right, my dear sweet brother-in-law, keep your mouth shut," said Christina.

Just then Percival announced the arrival of Mr. Anderson. As he came in, he suggested they all enter the dining room and be seated. He requested the presence of Percival and his wife Millie, and the two maids, Jean and Clair.

When they were all seated, he opened the official envelope and began to read:

I, Francene Michele Couquet, being of sound mind: To my beloved nephews, John Paul and Louis Alexander, and my beloved niece Michele Lynn, I leave $10,000 each. This money will be revoked, if after this day, they should

return to this house or prop-
erty.

To the town of Pilar, I leave
$60,000 to help cover ex-
penses for the much needed
supplies for the hospital.

To my faithful servants,
Percival and Millie, I leave the
Servants' House and a substantial lifelong income if they
will agree to continue their
services to my house and
grounds. This income will
include enough to pay for
gardeners and any up-keep
expenses necessary to keep

the Couquet prestige in Pilar.

To Jean and Clair, I leave an income for life, if they too, will agree to stay on, to do their respective duties.

And last, to my cat, I leave this house and the rest of my fortune. He is to have the run of the complete house, and from 9:00pm until 9:00am, no one is to step foot in this house. No matter what hap-pens or what the circum-stances may be, these are the conditions. This means my four servants, Clair, Jean, Percival, and Millie are to overlook anything that happens here after 9:00pm. This may seem a strange request, but I know they will honor it.

And so it was. The disgruntled relatives left, never to return, and the servants went about their respective duties.

Chapter 3

That night, at precisely 8:45pm, the servants locked the proud and noble mansion and went to their meager abode.

Percival invited Jean and Clair to stay downstairs in their apartment and join them for a glass of brandy. As he poured the drinks, he started talking of the strange events that had taken place that morning.

"What do you suppose Madame Couquet meant by us not returning to the house until 9 o'clock in the morning?"

Clair had been very quiet all day, but now she spoke. "It certainly is weird, but as for me, I am very pleased with this setup and don't intend to do anything to make her unhappy. In these 30 years that we have served her, I'm sure you'll agree that strange things did happen. I can't help but think that if we don't honor her wishes, she will have some way of knowing."

They all nodded in agreement. Millie got up to let her cat out. She had been pacing by the door since they came in.

"That cat is certainly restless tonight. I've never seen her quite like this before."

Percival just laughed and said, "Yes, maybe she's anxious to get out and see her boyfriend."

Jean remarked, "I'd laugh if she struck up a relationship with Madame Couquet's cat. After all, she's a full-blooded Persian, and he's just an alley cat."

Millie laughed, "He may be just an alley cat, but he's the only millionaire cat I know!"

Percival said, "Maybe she was eaves dropping when Mr. Anderson read the will."

The clock on the wall began to chime. They all sat in silence and counted, 1-2-3-4-5-6-7-8-9. The hair on the backs of their necks seems to creep, although they didn't understand why. Jean and Clair said goodnight and went upstairs to their own apartment.

Outside, the roar of an engine filled the air. That beautiful sports car that Madame Couquet had purchased two months ago pulled out of the driveway. Jean heard the noise and looked out of the up-stairs window. "Look!" she hollered, "Someone is stealing Madame Couquet's car."

Clair ran to the window, "He looks like a handsome man. Do you think Louis came back to get the car?"

"I don't think he would have nerve enough after what his aunt said in the will. With that money-hungry wife of his, I'm sure he wouldn't take a chance on losing the $10,000 just for a fancy sports car."

"I think you're right about that, but that definitely was not John."

"Maybe we better call the police."

"Let's wait and talk to Percy in the morning. I have a very funny feeling about this."

Jean nodded, and they both retired to their rooms.

Chapter 4

The night air was fresh and clean. It was a beautiful night for a walk. Jolene strolled down the road toward town. As she quietly walked in her cat-like fashion, she suddenly heard the roar of an engine, and the screeching halt of breaks. She turned and saw a handsome stranger in a red Jaguar. He pulled over to the side and said, "Are you going into town?"

Very nervously, she answered, "Yes I am."

"Hop in. I'll drive you there."

"No thanks. I never ride with strangers."

"Well, my name is Jordan Couquet. What's yours?"

"I'm Jolene Du Bois."

"Now that we know each other, I guess we're not strangers anymore."

As Jolene reluctantly climbed into the car, she said, "Are you any relation to Madame Francene Couquet?"

"Well, sort of. Why do you ask? Did you know her?"

"In a way. She was always very kind to me."

"Did you know her well?"

"I guess as well as anyone did."

The ride into town made Jolene quite nervous. She was not used to traveling at such speeds, nor was she keen on the idea of being picked up by a stranger.

There it was! Alfonso's, the restaurant she'd heard so much about. He'd stopped the car right in front. As he took the keys out of the ignition, he said, "Won't you join me for dinner and a drink?"

Jolene was still quite reluctant of this fast-moving character, but thinking of his family name, she figured it wouldn't be too bad to join him for a little socializing.

Jordan was the perfect gentle-man. He'd ordered Manhattans before dinner and shrimp cocktail as an appetizer. He gave her the prerogative of ordering soup and salad. Digging into the filet mignon, she smiled. He certainly did have exquisite taste. When was the last time she'd felt this way about anyone? She couldn't remember. She then decided she'd hook her claws into this one and never let him go.

After the exclusive dinner, they headed toward the discotheque. The go-go dancers were pretty wild, and the noise was almost unbearable. Jolene felt quite out of place here but did not want to say anything to hurt Jordan's feelings. It didn't take them too long to get into the swing of things. They talked with some of the members of the jet-set. Jolene was still uncertain of this type of night life. Jordan seemed to be enjoying himself, but Jolene couldn't help thinking this might be just a big front.

They left at about 2:00am and started walking to the car. Jordan suddenly broke the new silence, "It was very nice of you to join me tonight. Where can I drop you off?"

Jolene's heart sank. "The Hotel Royale would be just fine." She had seen the sign when they first got into town and thought this would be a good place to stay."

Jordan silently turned the car in that direction. He wondered if he would ever see this lovely girl again.

He pulled up in front of the Hotel Royale and seemed to have his mind a million miles away. Finally, he said, "Jolene, will you be free tomorrow night? I mean, would you like to go to a movie?"

Jolene thought a moment. "Yes, I would love to. Would 9:30pm be alright?"

"That would be fine. What room are you staying in? I'll phone you."

"Oh! Uh . . . that won't be necessary. I'll be ready."

Jordan gave her a light kiss on her nose and said good night.

It seemed like a long drive home, and Jordan had an empty, lonely feeling for the first time in his life. He'd felt almost the same when Madame Couquet had died, but somehow, this was even worse.

When he walked into the house, it seemed darker and lonelier than he'd ever remembered. He sat down in his favorite easy chair and thought to himself. He wondered how long he'd be able to keep his secret from Jolene and what she would do if she knew the truth about him. Was he being fair to her by deceiving her this way? Was this a wonderful, magical spell that Madame Couquet had bestowed upon him? Or was this a horrible, nightmarish curse?

With these thoughts swirling around in his head, he fell asleep.

Chapter 5

Jolene stood in front of the hotel after Jordan had driven off. Here she was in this town that she'd only seen from the car window before this night. What could she do? She couldn't go home . . . not yet anyway. She looked into the purse she was carrying and found some money. Madame Couquet had even taken care of that little detail.

After thinking it over for a minute, she walked into the hotel and very shyly to the desk. The old man looked up over his glasses at her. This look scared her a little, but then he said, "May I help you miss?"

"Yes, sir. I would like a room"

"I hate to turn such a pretty girl away, especially so late, but the only room that's empty is re-served."

"Well, couldn't I have the room just until 8:00am?"

"Sorry, but the lady called three

weeks ago and made the reser-
vation. She also paid for two
months in advance."

"Well, I really have no place to
go, and if the room is empty . . . "

"I'd really like to help you out,
but Madame Couquet was well
known around here, and I promised I would hold this room until
a Miss Jolene Du Bois came in."

"But I am Jolene Du Bois!"

"Why didn't you say so to begin
with? Come along, and I'll show
you to your room."

They walked down the narrow
corridor until they came to room

number 9. "Here's your room, and here's your key. Now have a good night's sleep."

Jolene called down the hall to him, "Would you please have the desk ring me at 8:00am sharp?"

"Yes, Miss. We'll be happy to do that for you."

Now she was alone to think of this wild thing that was actually happening to her. It was just too hard to believe. She began wondering about Jordan. Why hadn't she ever seen him at the mansion, if he was indeed related to Madame Couquet? The only Jordan she'd ever heard of, was that awful cat that chased her up the tree once.

Could this be the same Jordan? Of course! That was it. She giggled to herself, "Madame Couquet certainly did see to every detail."

Now she wouldn't have to worry about Jordan finding out about her little secret. She thought about it for a while and decided not to tell him right away. It might be fun to let him wonder a little bit. She would become a mystery to him. That would pay him back for startling her so much that day he chased her up the tree.

Jolene fell asleep quite satisfied with her decision.

* * *

The phone was ringing. Jolene opened her eyes and picked up the receiver. "Hello?" she said sleepily.

"Its 8:00am Miss Du Bois."

"Thank you very much."

Jolene dressed quickly and left the hotel. As she walked toward the mansion at the edge of town, she wondered if she had left herself enough time. She couldn't remember how far it was. If she could just make it as far as the long driveway, she'd be safe. No one would be around to see her.

There it was. She checked her watch, 8:45. *That's good*, she thought. It's a half hour walk. She strolled up the driveway very slowly. She stopped by the big tree and waited. As she looked up at the tree, she laughed to herself. This was the very tree that Jordan had chased her up last summer.

The door of the servants' house opened. Percival called, "Here kitty, kitty. There you are! Where have you been? You've never stayed out all night before."

Millie patted Jolene on the head

and gave her some milk and her favorite food. "If you don't behave yourself, we'll have to keep you in at night." Jolene purred and wondered if she really meant that.

Jean and Clair came downstairs and told Percival about the sports car disappearing. He went to the window, "Well, the car is there now. Remember we are to overlook everything that happens after 9:00pm. It does seem strange, but we must respect her wishes."

The servants left for the mansion at 9:15am, figuring it would be safe to enter. As they walked into the living room, they found Jordan curled up in the easy chair, still asleep. Millie called to Jordan to come and have his milk and tuna. This had always been his favorite breakfast. Jordan walked slowly into the kitchen. He lapped up a little milk and went back to the living room. He hopped up on the large sill that was padded nicely with big cushions. He gazed out of the window, with a sad, dejected expression.

Millie came in and sat next to him. She patted him on his head, "Poor Jordan, you look so lonely.

You must really miss Madame Couquet." Jordan looked up at her and purred a little. He wanted to show his appreciation to this kind woman, even though she didn't understand his true feelings.

Chapter 6

This second day of the spell seemed very long to Jordan. He thought of what Madame Couquet had told him. He'd remembered something about 9 days. What had she said? Would this spell last only 9 days? No! That wasn't it. Something special would happen at the end of 9 days. He wondered what she had meant by that.

Now he began to think of his date tonight with Jolene. She was a most mysterious girl. He should have insisted on knowing her room number, but then here it was 6:00pm. Only three more hours, and the magic would begin again.

A few times during the day, he'd looked out of the window and had seen Percival's cat. She was by far the prettiest cat he'd ever seen. The way she walked! It was almost familiar to him. He'd thought of the time he tried to make friends with her, but she ran up a big tree. Maybe if she realized his true intentions, she would be friendlier.

The longer Jordan thought of it, the more he wanted to make friends with her. *Tomorrow,* he thought. *I'll go out there and try again*. After all, his hours at night are reserved for Jolene, but this could make the day go faster and be more interesting. He felt better already. Being quite satisfied with his decision, he headed into the kitchen. There was Millie. He rubbed her leg and the refrigerator. "Jordan, you look much better. Maybe you'll eat something now."

Millie put fresh food and milk down for him, and he ate like it was his last meal. Now he washed and jumped up on the easy chair. He would take a little cat nap before his extraordinary change took place.

The servants locked up the mansion in good time, to retire to their own cozy little home. They felt more relaxed now and paid little attention to the big mansion.

Mille let Jolene out again. She'd been meowing so loud, they just couldn't stand it any longer. Percival told Jolene that if she wanted to stay out all night again, it was her own reputation she'd have to live down. Percival was quite comical at times, and Jolene really loved him for it. Before she left, she promised herself she would not do anything that might hurt these wonderful people. *If they only knew,* she thought. *But then some day, maybe they will.*

Jolene scampered down the driveway as fast as her little legs could carry her. She figured she could travel much faster as a cat and wouldn't get so tired. Besides, she'd be an awful lot safer. She was pretty lucky that it was Jordan who had picked her up the night before. She kept on running until she reached the edge of town. She stopped right by the stone wall and waited. This will be a very good spot to wait for the change to take place. It was only a five minute walk to the hotel from here, and that would give her plenty of time to get ready for Jordan to pick her up.

Jolene walked very nonchalantly into the hotel and down the hallway to her room. She went in and turned the lights on. It was a very lovely room. She hadn't really taken the time to look it over. She walked over to the closet and opened the sliding doors. There she saw the most beautiful wardrobe a girl could ever hope to own. There were dresses, suits, gowns, something for every occasion that might come up.

After looking over the clothes and shoes, she decided that the light green pants suit would be just the thing to wear to a movie. She dressed quickly and fixed her hair and makeup. Five more minutes, and Jordan would be there. She picked up a magazine and started thumbing through it. Just then, there was a light knock at the door. When she opened it, there stood Jordan. He was as handsome as she had remembered.

"Hi, beautiful," he said.

"You're early."

"I just couldn't wait another five minutes to see that lovely face of yours."

"Oh come now, flattery will get you, uh . . . everywhere."

"Okay, let's go. We should be just in time for the next show at the Palace."

NINE

They walked outside, entered the gorgeous red Jaguar, and headed down the road. Soon they saw the bright lights of the Palace. On the marquis was the title of the movie they were about to see. Jolene thought it was a strange title, "Cat O' Nine Tails."

The movie was over shortly before midnight. They agreed that it was a spine tingler. Jolene had covered her eyes a few times, and Jordan reassured her. "It's all staged! There's nothing to worry about."

When they walked out in the

cool night air, Jordan asked her, "Would you like to top the evening off with a night cap?"

"I'd love to, but if it's all the same to you, I would prefer a little quieter place tonight."

"Just what I had in mind."

"That looks like a nice place right across the street. The music coming from there seems to be more on the gentle side, mood music; I guess you'd call it."

"Then that's the place for us, because baby, I'm in the mood."

They walked across the street and entered the Silver Gate. The hostess greeted them and showed them to a nice little table in the corner. The lights were low, and the only sounds were soft whispers and music. This was the perfect place for lovers to meet.

Jordan took the liberty of ordering the drinks. As they slowly sipped their drinks, they sat staring into each others eyes.

"Jolene, there is something I really should tell you but I just don't know where to start."

"I know just what you're going to say. You're not human."

"What?"

"I mean, how can anyone as superb a specimen as you be human?"

"Oh, come now Jolene, you're just toying with me."

"No! I'm quite serious. I have never seen a man, in all my life, quite as handsome as you are."

"Now it's my turn; flattery will get you uh . . . everywhere."

Chapter 7

After sitting there in the Silver Gate and discussing every subject they could think of, the hostess came over with the check. "I'm sorry to disturb you two lovebirds, but by law we do have to close."

Jordan got up, and being the perfect gentleman, he pulled out the chair for Jolene. He paid the check, and they left this wonderful place where they had both felt so at ease. Jordan, not wanting to break this new-found magic spell, suggested they go for a short ride. Jolene was not averse to this, so she mentioned driving down to the lake. With the wind blowing in her long beautiful hair, and the moonlight shining in her eyes, she felt like a special angel.

Jordan stopped the car at the edge of the lake. This was by far the most wonderful evening he could ever remember. They sat silently, for what seemed like an eternity. Then he broke the silence with, "Jolene, I think I've fallen in love with you."

"Oh, Jordan, I hope that's true. I hope it is not just because of the unusual circumstances tonight."

"This is very bad, and I really have no right to love you. I have an unbelievable background, and only lady luck has shined down on me."

"I don't want to hear any more about it right now, so please just take me home and let me think."

Jordan took his time driving back to the hotel. When he stopped the car, he jumped out and ran around to open the door for Jolene. He walked with her to her door. She found her key and unlocked the door. Suddenly, he took her in his arms and kissed her good night. Before Jolene came back to her senses, he was gone. She went into her room in a very dreamy mood. She sat down at her dressing table and looked in the mirror. Now she felt a little ashamed that she hadn't told Jordan that she knew about his secret and that she shared the same.

She got undressed and put on her night gown. When she walked over to the bed, she noticed an addition to the room. There on the night stand was an alarm clock. She set the alarm for 8:00 and hoped that four hours would be enough sleep. She snuggled down and closed her eyes, but somehow sleep did not come easily tonight. She got up and opened her window. She thought this way, she'd still be able to get home if she overslept. Now with a renewed confidence, she finally dozed off.

Chapter 8

Jordan drove home very cautiously. He couldn't get Jolene out of his mind. It kept coming back to him, what she had said about his not being human. He wondered if she could possibly have some uncanny way of knowing, or if she was really just joking. These thoughts kept going through his mind until he found himself unlocking the door to the mansion. It scared him a little, since he didn't even remember getting home.

He took out a bottle of wine and sat down. He thought maybe a few glasses of wine would make him fall asleep more quickly. He had guessed right, because the next thing he heard was the voices of the servants. Clair seemed excited about something. He came to his senses and listened to what she was saying.

"See? I knew someone was in this house again last night. Here is a dirty wine glass still sitting here, and nearly a half a bottle gone."

Jordan decided to be more careful of picking up after himself.

"You're right as usual, Clair," remarked Jean. "But I can't for the life of me, think who could have been here."

Percival started in his usual comical tone, "Maybe there's a skeleton in the closet, or we might even be dealing with the super-natural!" He'd said that last part as if he half believed it himself.

"Oh Percy," retorted Millie, "you sure do have a way with words.

You're going to scare the daylights out of all of us; yourself included, I'm afraid."

"Well, you have to admit that these are the strangest goings on around here; more so than we have ever witnessed before."

Jean trembled at her next thought which she said aloud. "Do you think it's possible that Madame Couquet has returned from the grave to haunt us?"

"It's possible that she is sending back unknown materialistic events," said Percival, "but as for haunting us, personally I don't think that is her intention."

"Absolutely true. She would never do anything to harm us. We were the only ones to ever believe in her and her unusual ways." Millie said these words, half believing them and half hoping they were true. At least this statement was enough to ease their minds for a while.

Jordan wished there was some way he could convey a little reassurance to these dedicated people; yet something unexplainable told him that in due time, they would all come to know that these events were taking place for a specific purpose.

He felt that old familiar sensation of hunger coming on. He thought that it would take away the distraught feelings of the servants, if he could get their minds on something else. Millie was only too happy to oblige with a warm pat on the head, and a wonderful breakfast. "You definitely have a much better disposition today, Jordan," she said. "I only hope you continue to keep it."

Chapter 9

After his substantial nourish-
ment, Jordan felt like a new man
. . . er . . . cat. He sauntered over
to the door and meowed to go out.
Reminding himself of his decision
of yesterday, he walked out into
the garden. The air was sweet and
fresh, and he figured he'd be very
cool about his actions. When he

reached the end of the path, he looked around to see if there were any signs of that splendid cat of Percy's. Upon surveying the entire area, and receiving no clues as to her whereabouts, he resolved to catch a butterfly. *These little butterflies certainly are tricky,* he thought. After chasing them for a while and ending up with only a nose full of fragrant flowers, he decided to look for some birds.

Ah! There's a pair of unsuspecting bluebirds. He stalked quietly through the brush until he was just about on them. Just as he

took a flying leap at them, they
were off to a safer spot. *What
rascals! They must have seen me
coming and waited just long
enough to tease me!*

Right at that moment, a new
form appeared at the edge of the
garden. Jordan's heart sank; there
she was in all of her radiant glory.
He watched her move in her grace-
ful manner. He could think of only
one other creature as breathtaking
as she appeared, and that was
Jolene. As he watched her me-
ander through the garden, he
compared her gait to that of

Jolene's. Every movement she made seemed to be more and more similar to that of the one he loved. Could it be possible that they were one and the same? Or was it just his own hopeful imagination? He decided to confront her with his suspicion; this female animal who was tantalizing him with every movement of her gorgeous body. Without thinking any further, he bounded away into her direction. She looked up from her concerned concentration and saw him coming. Immediately she took off like a flash and reached home safely.

He dared not enter the same window into which she had disappeared. His conclusion to this incident was that if this was in fact Jolene, she would not have run away so persistently.

Jolene, once inside, felt a great relief that he had not followed her.

Chapter 10

The rest of the day passed without further incident. The eventful phenomena took place as it had the two previous nights.

Here was Jordan, all set for a night on the town, but realizing he had failed to make a date with Jolene. He sat in confused disarray.

Jolene on the other hand, sat nervously in her hotel room wondering if he would call. To her amazement, the phone rang just at the precise second she'd though this. By the time the ringing registered, it had already rung for the third time.

"Hello?"

"Miss Du Bois?"

"Yes."

"We have a call for you. I'll connect you right away."

The voice on the line was the one and only voice she wanted to hear. "Jolene? This is Jordan."

"Hi. How are you?"

"At this moment I'm very lonely.

NINE

But it eases the tension just to hear your voice."

"I'm glad you called. I was just thinking about you."

"I was wondering if I might . . . uh . . . pick you up and go for a little spin around town."

"Oh Jordan, I would really love to, but I am kind of tired tonight." She thought a little white lie wouldn't hurt at this point and might keep him interested.

"I'm sorry to hear that! Would you like to make it tomorrow night instead?"

"Yes, that would be fine. You can

pick me up at the usual time tomorrow night."

After hanging up, Jolene felt thankful that she hadn't made him lose interest completely. Now she couldn't decide what to do to pass the long hours away.

She made up her mind to take a long walk around town and acquaint herself with the surroundings. She dressed in a not-too sexy, not-too basic outfit and left the hotel. As she walked coyly down the street, she took the time to look at the merchandise on display in every window. As she

crossed the street and began walking up the other side, she heard a
very shrill wolf whistle. Her reaction was that of mixed emotions.
One part of her felt excited and
proud, but the other part felt very
nervous. She ignored the whistle
and continued walking in her
exclusive way.

A few times, Jolene stopped and
looked in the windows of dress
shops. She walked into the drug
store on the corner and browsed
through the paperbacks. After
selecting one which she thought
might interest her, she purchased

it and walked outside. Starting across the street toward the hotel, she almost stepped into the path of a car.

"Hi honey," the voice called.

It was Jordan!

"Boy, you surely gave me a start! Do you always have to drive so fast?"

"I wasn't going fast. You stepped out in traffic without looking. You know if you were a cat, you'd only have eight lives left." Jordan had said that as if he were testing her.

"You're absolutely right," she said, wondering if maybe he did suspect something. Changing the subject as fast as she could, she continued, "I was just heading back to my room to settle down with a good book."

"You sure you won't change your mind and go for a spin?"

"Well, only if you promise to get me back early. The old man in the hotel is beginning to give me funny looks, and I do have to think of my reputation."

"Anything you say. Just to be with you for a few minutes will make this trip into town worthwhile."

"You say such flattering things. You make it awfully easy for a girl to fall in love with you." She got into the car, and he drove off toward the lake.

"I hope you mean that Jolene, because by now you know how I feel about you."

Chapter 11

Jordan stopped the car in a romantic spot near the lake. "Jolene, I'd like to know a little more about you. Would you mind a few personal questions?"

"Not at all." She figured she could be vague in answering anything that seemed too delicate.

"Have you always lived here in Pilar?"

"No, I was born in Jarvis. That's about twenty miles south of here."

"You seem so well bred. Do you have any relatives living in Pilar?"

"In a way. You probably know Percival and Millie Du Bois."

"Yes, I've known them for years!"

"They are the only relatives I have near here."

"Then that must be how you knew Madame Couquet."

"That's true. I met her through them." She continued, "She was the most fabulous person I have ever known."

"She certainly was. She treated me as if I were her very own son. After my background, I give her a lot of credit for refining me."

"If your life before you met her was as bad as you say, I guess she could really be proud of you now."

"Well, if it hadn't been for her, I'd probably have been just a bum roaming the streets."

"I guess you were right when you told me Lady Luck had shined down on you."

"Yes, you might even say that Lady Luck is named Francene Michele Couquet."

"Jordan, I really don't want to cut short your questions, but I think I'd better go back to my room now."

"Okay Jolene, a promise is a promise." He started up the engine, and they were off again, headed for the Hotel Royale.

Jordan walked her to her door again and kissed her goodnight. Her head was really in a spin when he left. Now she felt guiltier than ever for not telling him about her secret. She even felt ashamed about avoiding him that morning. She settled down with her book but when she had finished the third chapter, she realized she didn't even know what she had read. All she could think about was Jordan. She wondered what his reaction would be when she finally did tell him what she knew. *Will he be angry?* She thought. *Or would he laugh it off?*

When she was finally able to put these thoughts out of her mind, she fell asleep.

Chapter 12

Jordan started to head for home. When he reached the edge of town and the driveway to the mansion, he continued driving in a southerly direction toward the town of Jarvis. He decided he wanted to see this little town where Jolene had been born. The town was peaceful and quiet and resembled its twin, Pilar, very much. He drove through the main street to the outskirts, then turned around and headed back to Pillar.

The thing that had impressed him the most, were the two regal mansions at the entrance to Jarvis. He thought to himself, *With Jolene's mannerisms, one must belong to her family.* Much to his surprise, neither one said Du Bois. On the large front gate of one was a plaque reading, J. C. Pilar, and the other, R. F. Jarvis.

Coming back toward Pilar, he noticed a sign that said Le Petite Chalet, and set back on the hill was a beautiful little restaurant. He made up his mind that this is where he'd take Jolene on their next date.

Driving his car after seeing Jolene had not proved too wise. He always seemed to have his mind on her instead of the road. Tonight was the payoff. Before he knew what happened, he saw the blinding headlights coming right at him! He swerved and missed the car by a fraction of an inch. The sound of the horn was still echoing in his ears when he pulled to the side of the road.

"That was close," he said aloud, "and I was in the wrong. I didn't realize I was on the other side of the road. Well, only eight more lives for me!"

Jordan was very cautious now. This time he did not pass the drive-way but turned in and drove up to the carport outside the front door of the mansion. He entered the dark vestibule with a very shaky feeling. It had not left him since his narrow escape from what could have been a fatal accident. He became more nervous as he thought of the fact that he could have taken his own life plus that of an innocent person.

Jordan turned on some lights and went to the refrigerator. He took out what was left of the wine he'd opened the night before and sat down to indulge in a little relaxation. Without thinking, he picked up the phone and dialed the number for the Hotel Royale. "Room 9 please." He said when the ringing had stopped.

The voice on the other send sounded sleepy. "Hello?"

"Jolene! I hope I didn't wake you up."

"You did but I don't mind."

"I just wanted to say goodnight again, and I'm sending this kiss."

"That's very sweet of you Jordan. Here is one in return."

After washing his wine glass, Jordan went up the long staircase to retire. The wine worked swiftly and soon Jordan was in dreamland. His dreams were a weird combination of Jolene and that Persian cat of Percy's. First, Jolene would be her beautiful self. Then she would turn into that lovely cat. Back and forth through his dream, they continued to change until he awoke in a cold sweat. *Wow!* He thought. *I must be subconsciously wishing this were true.*

Until morning, Jordan slept and woke in very much the same order.

Chapter 13

Jolene was awake at the crack of dawn. She got up cheerfully and dressed. She made her bed and straightened her room. She decided it would be a good idea to pick out her outfit for tonight.

She picked out the white knit bell bottoms and matching bolero. There were tiny yellow, pink, and blue flowers embroidered down the sides of the legs and around the bolero. She wondered which matching satin blouse she liked best. She finally decided that the pink one flattered her complexion better than the yellow or blue. After picking out the stylish white sandals and matching little purse, she laid out the entire ensemble on her bed. She was very pleased with her choice and admired Madame Couquet's elegant taste.

She left her room in time to return to the manor before the change took place.

Millie was calling to her just as

she emerged from the bushes.

"Here kitty, kitty. Oh, there you

are. What is the matter with you?

Lately you disappear at night and

don't show up until breakfast

time!"

Jolene put on her great act to

soften Millie, which was not very

hard to do. Millie had a heart that

was easily softened by such a

beautiful cat. After feeding Jolene,

she left for her chores at the

mansion.

Jordan was in pretty good humor

this morning and really hammed it

up for the servants. He started off

with his normal ritual of purring and rubbing against everything within reach. He loved being the center of attention, and being able to con Millie into feeding him was the ultimate of his goals. What a great job of putting her on he did. He had the knack down pat after all these years. First, he would rub against her legs, then the refrig- erator, and then back to her legs again. By the time he finished with her, she figured he was dying of hunger.

While Jordan was enjoying his meal, which consisted of tuna and milk, he heard a knock at the front door. He left his dishes to go into the living room to see what it was all about. Percival invited the unexpected guest into the house. Jordan listening intently as the man spoke. "Well, Percival, I have known you for a number of years. You are a very trustworthy person. We of the town know that Madame Couquet has entrusted her entire estate to you and the rest of the staff."

"That is true Mr. Folstein."

"Then I must ask you if you have noticed anything strange going on at the mansion each night."

"I haven't noticed anything out of the ordinary but I will keep an eye out if you think it's necessary."

"Yes, I'm inclined to think so. Some of the folks in town have seen a red sports car just like the one outside. I, for one, thought it was foolish of Francene to buy it when she did but there were times when she was quite eccentric."

"Come to think of it, she did mention before she died that a young fellow had her permission to use the car and house at his discrepancy." Percival hoped Mr.

Folstein could not see through this little white lie. "So like I said before, none of us has seen anything out of the ordinary."

"That's very strange! Did she tell you anything about this young man?"

"No. Not a thing. I was never one to pry into her personal matters. If she said it's alright, then I see no reason to question the situation."

"Well, if you say so. Thank you for your time, Percival. Now I can go back and set the town at ease. They have always been very foolish with their talk of witchcraft and other nonsense."

"Well, I served her for thirty years, along with my wife and the two maids. And to my recollection, she had been nothing but good to us. So if she was a witch, she was a good one," Percival laughed as he said this.

"I know what you mean. Sorry to have troubled you."

Percival showed him out, and after he was out of sight, he closed the door and stood there in puzzlement. Jordan walked over and rubbed Percival's legs. He bent

down and petted him on the head.
"I don't know about you Jordan.
Somehow I get the feeling that
you're thanking me for what I
said." This had been Jordan's main
concern.

Percival got up and went to the
kitchen to find Millie. He wanted to
ask her if he'd done the proper
thing by telling a fib to Mr.
Folstein. By the time he reached
the kitchen, he had made up his
mind. Instead of feeling guilty
about it, he felt as if he'd done
something good. *This must be a
sign that I did the right thing,* he

thought.

Millie asked, "Who was at the door Percy?"

"It was Mr. Folstein, the mayor from Pilar."

"Did he want anything important?"

"No, he just wondered about the car being in town at night."

"What did you tell him?" asked Millie, with a worried sound to her voice.

"I told him everything was alright and not to think anything of it."

"That's good. I hope he doesn't

come back because I don't know how to explain it."

"I doubt if he'll return."

Chapter 14

Jordan was very relieved at what Percival had told the mayor. Now, he wouldn't have to worry at all about being seen. He tried to think of what he might say if someone stopped him and asked questions. *Oh, this is ridiculous,* he thought. *They probably won't ask questions, and if they do, I'll answer the best way I can.*

Since it was now raining, Jordan decided to stay in and look for something to do. He wandered from room to room until he spotted Jean. She was sitting in the library knitting on her sweater. Jordan hopped up on the sofa next to her. He watched her hands moving swiftly and the ball of yarn spinning on the floor. Being in a very playful mood, he jumped down and landed right on the yarn. He batted it with his front paws. Then he rolled over on his back and kicked it. Jean couldn't help but laugh at the tangled mess. Here was this full-grown cat, acting just like a kitten. She reached down and began to unwind the yarn from him. "You certainly look foolish with that yarn wrapped around you," she said.

When she finally got Jordan all unwound, he fled for another room. This time it was the den. Clair was just dusting the furniture with her feather duster. He hopped up on the desk and slapped at it. Clair laughed, "No, no, silly Jordan. This isn't a bird!" She played with Jordan for a few minutes. Then she said, "Okay dear, that's enough.

It's time I break for lunch, and I'm sure you must be hungry too. Let's go see if Millie has our food ready."

Jordan followed her to the kitchen. Millie was just dishing out the stew. It sure did smell good. They all sat down and began to eat. Percival looked down at Jordan, who was sitting there tipping his head from side to side. "Come up here next to me, Jordan." Percy patted the seat as he said this.

Millie got up and dished out a small bowl of meat and gravy for Jordan, and placed it on the table in front of him. Jordan looked at her and then very politely, put his front paws on the table and began to eat. He thought to himself, *these people are certainly nice to me. No wonder Madame Couquet thought so much of them.*

When they were all finished eating, Jordan jumped down and washed himself like a good cat should. Millie, Jean, and Clair all pitched in and cleared the table. They worked together in harmony and got the kitchen in ship shape order in nothing flat. Jordan thought it was really amazing how well they got along with each other. In the few short years that he'd been there, they had never disagreed on anything. To be able to live together for thirty years and never so much as have a little spat must be some kind of a record. Wouldn't it be great if people all over the world could be like them? This would really be too much to ask for.

Jordan rested for the remainder of the day. At supper, he ate lightly, because he wanted to dine out with Jolene later.

Shortly before nine, the servants

left to return again the next morning.

Jolene had gone through her ritual again and was already on her way to the hotel. She'd be ready and waiting by the time Jordan picked her up.

Chapter 15

Jolene dressed in her white pants suit that she had picked out earlier that day. She looked very stunning when she answered the door. Jordan told her of his plans for an exciting evening. "We'll start off with dinner at a charming little restaurant I discovered."

"Sounds great!"

Jordan couldn't help himself as he kissed her on the forehead. "You look absolutely gorgeous tonight, darling."

"Thank you, sir."

Before long, they reached the little chalet with the appropriate French name. Once inside, they were taken aback by the truly exquisite atmosphere.

After the waitress brought their Manhattans, they sat quietly gazing into each other's eyes. Before they had much chance to talk, she was back with their order. They ate slowly, savoring every bite. Lobster was now at the top of Jolene's list of great foods to eat. They finished their meal and talked quietly about their chance meeting.

Jordan finally said, "Well, Jolene, how about making the evening complete with a night cap at my place?"

"That sounds wonderful."

Jordan paid the check, and they left the little cuisine. The parking lot attendant remembered which car they had come in and before Jordan could hand him the ticket, the car was in front of him.

"That's some beautiful machine you have there, sir!"

"Thank you. It's the only one like it. This little baby was custom built inside and out."

After tipping the young man, they were off with a roar down the hill.

"Jordan, please don't drive so fast. I get very nervous."

"I'm sorry," he said as he slowed down. "You know, Jolene, I have only known you for four days, and it seems like I've known you forever."

"I know what you mean. I feel the same way."

Jordan was driving very sanely now. When he got to the curve where he'd almost had the accident, his heart sank. He'd always remember that spot.

Soon they were in the drive that wound around to the big mansion. He drove up to the carport and stepped out. After opening the door for Jolene, he led her up the steps to the enormous front porch. He unlocked the door and turned on some lights. Jolene was stricken with wonder at the beauty of the vestibule. The sculptures and paintings seemed to belong to a museum rather than a private home. The lighting made everything seem to jump out at her and oh, so real.

Upon entering the living room, she was shocked at the enormity of it. The plush carpet, the stone fireplace that ran the length of one wall, the furniture! She was even awed by the huge crystal chande-lier. All this luxury was almost too much to imagine.

Chapter 16

Jordan had gone to the wall opposite the fireplace. As he pushed a button, the bar slowly turned into the room, and soft music began to play. He poured two drinks and brought one to Jolene. "Is scotch okay?"

"Uh . . . yes, that's fine."

Jordan suddenly noticed her amazed glassy stare. "What's

wrong, honey?"

"Oh nothing. I just had no idea this place was so . . . so gorgeous!"

They sat down on the sofa and simultaneously put their drinks on the coffee table.

"I was under the impression that you'd been here before."

"No, never inside."

"Well, then how did you meet Madame Couquet?"

"Oh! When she had gone over to see Percival and Millie."

"Then I guess that's why I don't remember seeing you around here before."

"That's right. You know, I really had a lot of respect for Madame Couquet. She was the only one who could ever really communicate with me."

"You mean you were a problem child?"

"I guess you might say that."

"Boy, you certainly have some vague answers!" Jordan had said this just as he got up to fix two more drinks.

When he came back and put the drinks on the table, he grabbed Jolene and kissed her. It all happened so fast. It really stunned her. Without thinking, she said, "Jordan, I know now that I have fallen in love with you. I guess there's no sense in kidding you any longer."

"What do you mean by that?"

"Well, I have been playing a sort of a game with you."

"So don't keep me in suspense. Let me hear all about it." Jordan wondered now what was in store for him.

"Well, remember that first night you picked me up?"

"I don't believe I could ever

forget."

"After you dropped me off at the hotel, I got to thinking."

"Yes, go on!"

"Well, I figured that, since the only Jordan I had ever heard of was Madame Couquet's cat, then it had to be you . . . transformed."

"How could you possibly know?" Jordan was taken aghast by that last statement.

"I'm surprised you haven't figured it out before this. I am Jolene!"

"I know that, but . . . "

"Haven't you ever heard my

name being called? Wait a minute!
You probably didn't. They always
say "Here, kitty, kitty!""

"You mean you're . . . Percival's
cat?"

"That's right!"

"And you knew since the first
night?"

"Uh huh."

"When I think of what I've been
going through! I've been half out of
my mind wondering how I could
tell you I'm a cat."

"Don't be angry with me Jordan.
It was only a joke."

"I'm not sure I can ever trust

you knowing you lied to me! Maybe this is all a big mistake!"

Jolene ran to the window and stood there sobbing. "I only did it to get even."

"Even for what?"

"For that time when you chased me up the tree."

"Well, dear, if that's all . . ."

"All, nothing! You really had me scared to death!"

"I was only trying to make friends."

"How was I supposed to know that?"

Jordan walked over and put his

arm around her. "Come on now. Sit down and finish your drink."

"I shouldn't even speak to you anymore!"

"That's what I like . . . a girl with spunk."

Jordan tried to console her with a little kiss on her nose. "Now, now, you're the one that wanted to get even, and now we are."

They finished their drinks, and Jordan took her home.

"I'll see you tomorrow night." He said as he left her at the hotel.

"Don't be too sure."

Chapter 17

The next day was pretty much of a drag for both Jordan and Jolene. It was another early June rainy day. The day went by as did the previous four days. Here it was, the fifth day since the spell. Jordan wondered what the next four days would bring.

Jolene was thinking about what had happened last night. She was still uncertain of her feelings toward Jordan's reaction. She was mad at him, and yet she felt a deep love for him.

Jordan's mind seemed to be running on the same track. He was proud of himself for stating his mind, yet worried about her subtle disposition.

Jolene spent most of the day taking short cat naps. She couldn't seem to find a comfortable position for too long at a time. She made up her mind not to see Jordan that night. After all, she thought, he did say he wouldn't be able to trust me.

When the time came for returning to the hotel, Jolene started out.
As she got to the driveway beyond
the big trees, there was a sudden
downpour. She ran as fast as she
could to the big porch on the mansion. She didn't really want to get
wet, so she jumped up on the
porch swing and waited. After a
few minutes, she made up her
mind to give in and see Jordan
after all. Jolene got up and walked
over to the door and rang the bell.
When Jordan opened the door, he
didn't seem too surprised to see

her. "Hi, honey. I was expecting you."

"Well, I really didn't want to see you tonight but I didn't feel like walking into town in the rain."

"I'll be glad to drive you there if you like."

"I don't want to impose on you."

Jordan walked over and put his arm around her. "Oh, come on now. You know darn well you're not really made at me."

"Yes I am."

"Come on, I'll fix you a drink, and you'll forget all about your troubles."

NINE

"Okay, but then you can take me to the hotel, so long as you offered."

After a few drinks, Jolene was back to herself again. They were talking and laughing as they'd done before. The music was getting to both of them, and they danced the hours away. Jolene looked at the clock and saw that it was already past two in the morning. "Jordan, I think you'd better take me to the hotel now. It's really getting late."

"No it isn't. It's early! Early in the morning."

"Very funny! But I really

shouldn't stay out this late."

"Why not? You don't' have anyone to answer to."

"No, just my own conscience."

"Okay. I'll take you home after we have a little snack and another drink."

Jordan prepared some hors d'oeuvres and canapés.

As they sat and nibbled, Jordan asked, "Jolene, why don't you stay here instead of going to the hotel every night?"

"Only if we were married."

"Then let's get married."

"Hey, slow down. You move too

fast for me."

"Well, why not? It was pre-arranged, wasn't it?"

"What do you mean?"

"Well, Madame Couquet must have wanted it this way, or she wouldn't have put the spell on you too."

"I think you're right but don't we have to get blood tests and a license and things like that?"

"I'll tell you what, tomorrow night, we'll leave at 9:00pm and visit Dr. Ellison. He'll be able to tell us what has to be done."

"Okay, now how about taking

me to the hotel?"

"Anything you say, love!"

Chapter 18

The next night at 9:00pm sharp, Jolene and Jordan left the mansion and headed for town.

Jordan stopped in front of the little white house. The sign out front said Normand C. Ellison, M.D. As they walked into the waiting room, Jolene could feel herself shaking. An elderly man in a white shirt came in. "May I help you?

Jordan spoke right up. "Yes, sir, we would like to get married so we came for a blood test."

"Of course, come right this way."

When he was finished, the doctor told them they could obtain the license at the town hall in the morning.

"What time do they open?" asked Jordan.

"They open at 8:00am, so if you get there early, I am sure it won't take too long. I'll have the results of the blood tests by then, and I'll drop it off on my way to the hospital."

NINE

Jordan thanked him, and they left.

"That was easier than I thought it would be." He said.

All of a sudden, Jolene started to laugh.

"What on earth is so funny?"

"Nothing really. I was just thinking about tomorrow. I hope it doesn't take too long at the town hall. It would be pretty embarrass-ing if they were filling out papers and found two cats sitting there!"

Jordan laughed too when she said that.

"Where would you like to go

tonight? I think we should celebrate, don't you?"

"Yes, but first, I'd like to change into something more fitting the occasion."

Jordan took her to the hotel. "I'll be back in half an hour to pick you up."

"Okay, I'll be ready."

Jolene went to her room. She opened the closet and found just the dress she was looking for. It was a very elegant chiffon. The lavender shade was perfect for her complexion. After she washed and put her makeup on, she slipped into the dress. The long piece of chiffon from the right shoulder, she draped over her left shoulder and pinned it with a delicate gold brooch.

When she was ready, she walked down the hall to the lobby. Jordan was already there. He had gone home and changed into his black bell bottoms and pale lavender shirt. The deep purple tie and white belted jacket topped off his outfit perfectly.

When she got to him, he handed her the small white box he was holding. When she opened it, there was a beautiful orchid. He helped her pin it to the dress, and they were both surprised to see that the colors matched exactly.

As they walked toward the car, Jordan suggested they try the Silver Gate for dinner. Jolene was very pleased with his decision. She had really enjoyed the atmosphere there when they had stopped in for a drink. Jordan drove over to the front of the Silver Gate and stopped the car. When he opened the door for Jolene, she looked over toward the Palace.

"Cat O' Nine Tails" is still

playing," she said. "That certainly was a spine chiller."

"You're right! Next time we go to a movie, we'll have to check to see what it's about first."

As Jordan and Jolene entered the Silver Gate, the hostess greeted them. "You two look like you need a romantic table for two. I have just the right spot." She showed them to a small table in the corner of the dimly-lit dining room.

The waitress came and took their order after a few minutes. They finished their roast beef

dinner and strawberry short cake.
After they finished their coffee,
Jordan paid the check, and they
left the Silver Gate. Jordan drove
down by the lake again and sat
gazing up at the stars. After a few
minutes of silence, he reached into
his jacket pocket. He handed
Jolene a tiny white box and said,
"This should make it official."

When she opened the box, there
was a lovely diamond ring. "Oh,
Jordan. It's beautiful!"

He helped her put it on and said,
"It sparkles just like your eyes."

"How did you know what size?"

"Just a lucky guess."

Jordan gave her a very romantic kiss. Now it really was official. They would be married as soon as possible.

When Jordan dropped Jolene off at the hotel, he reminded her to be ready at 7:45am. "If we're the first ones at the town hall, maybe we can get out in time."

"Okay, dear, I'll be ready and waiting."

Chapter 19

Here it was, the seventh day since the spell began. Jordan got up early and dressed. He got into the car and drove to town. When he got to Jolene's hotel room, she was ready. They very nervously left for the town hall.

As they walked up the steps to the big doors, they noticed the sign:

Open
9:00am to 5:00pm Monday,

*Tuesday and Wednesday
8:00am to 4:00pm Thursday and
Friday
8:00am to 12:00pm Saturday*

"We're lucky today is Thursday," said Jordan. Just as he'd finished, the janitor came and unlocked the door.

They waited patiently by the sign that said "Marriage Licenses." The woman looked up from her desk. "Hi there. I'll be with you in just a moment. Please take a seat."

They sat for what seemed like hours, but when the woman spoke again, Jordan checked the clock. It was exactly 8:00am.

"My name is Mrs. Monroe."

After answering the seemingly endless questions, signing papers and having official stamps and signatures, Jordan paid the $2.00 fee, and they headed out of the building.

"We're fortunate it's only 8:30. We'll have just enough time to get back to the mansion."

When they reached the mansion, Jordan put the license in a safe place. Then he walked over and opened a window. "I think you'll be safer in here when the change takes place. No one will be able to see you, and you'll be able to get out through the window."

"That's a great idea."

Jordan kissed Jolene and said, "Tonight we'll make the plans for the wedding. Would you prefer a church wedding or a Justice of the Peace?"

"It really doesn't matter to me. When you're married, you're married!"

"That's true, and it doesn't matter to me either."

Soon they were both cats again. Jolene jumped out of the window and headed for home. Percival was there as usual and let her in. "I don't know what's come over you lately, Jolene. We never see you anymore."

Millie put her food down for her, and they all left for the big house. Jean noticed the opened window and immediately closed it. "I think it's going to get pretty hot today, Percy. Why don't you put the air conditioning unit on now?"

Percival put the air conditioning on, and they all checked through the house to make sure the rest of the windows were closed. The servants went about their duties as usual. They worked together and always kept the enormous place spotless. They were indeed fortunate people. Since they had worked for Madame Couquet, she had never given them an official day off. Yet they never complained. The agreement was that any time they needed personal days, they took as many as they needed and were still paid for them. One time Clair had gone back to Paris to visit her ailing mother. She returned two months later and was paid for the days she was absent. They had always worked as frequently or as little as they liked. Sometimes they would work along steadily for an hour, and then they would all rest for an hour. There were times when they even took a few hours to swim in the year-round pool. This was the one day when they all decided to cool off in the water.

Jordan watched as they splashed and fooled like a bunch of kids. This was one thing he'd forgotten about. As a cat, he naturally did not like the water but he wondered if he might like to swim as a person. He decided to check with Jolene tonight. Maybe she would enjoy a dip in the pool after they made the wedding plans. The more he watched the servants splashing around, the more he wanted to try it. *Yes*, he thought. *This is where we'll spend our time this evening.*

Chapter 20

Jolene didn't have to walk into town anymore. The only distance she had to walk now was to the mansion. When she rang the bell, Jordan was ready. He patted his jacket pocket to make sure he had the marriage license.

They climbed into the jaguar and started off toward Pilar. On the way, Jordan told her he'd thought it over and decided to see Parson Carter. "Since Madame Couquet was a member of his church, I think it's only proper that he would perform the ceremony."

"I'm glad you decided on a church wedding for something so sacred to both of us."

When they reached the home of Parson Carter, Jordan ran around and opened the door for Jolene. They walked up the front steps and rang the bell. A very pleasant-looking woman answered the door. She smiled as she greeted them. "Is the Reverend at home?" inquired Jordan.

"Yes. Won't you come in? I'll get him for you."

"Thank you," said Jordan politely.

When Parson Carter entered the room, they were filled with awe. He seemed like a quiet man and yet his kind face seemed to shout happiness to all who would see him.

"May I be of assistance?" he asked smiling.

"Yes, I think so," said Jordan. "We would like to get married. I have the license right here." He handed the official paper to the Parson.

"Of course . . . would you like a small wedding or were you thinking of a big to-do?"

"Well, if you have no objections, we would like to have your wife as a witness and would prefer to be married at night."

"Tomorrow night is out. We have a meeting of the church elders. Would Saturday night be okay?"

"That would be perfect! Can we make it at 9:30?"

"Yes, that is fine with me. That will give me plenty of time to finish preparing my sermon for Sunday Morning service."

"Okay, we'll see you at the church on Saturday night."

"Oh, and one more thing, you leave the license with me, and I can get everything ready."

When they got out to the car, Jordan suddenly realized he hadn't consulted Jolene through the whole conversation with the Parson.

"I hope Saturday is okay with you, dear."

"Well, if it wasn't, I would have said so. It just seems so unbelievable."

"I don't want to change the

subject but I wondered if you would like to come back to the house for a swim."

"That sounds great! Can you stop at the hotel first so I can get my suit?"

"Sure thing, honey."

Jolene was back in a flash with her bathing items. They headed back to the mansion and before they knew it, they were diving into the pool.

"Oh, Jordan. This is super! I never thought I would enjoy being in the water this much."

"Yeah! I guess being a "people" isn't so bad after all."

"You're a character."

After spending a couple of hours in the pool, they changed and met in the living room.

Jordan poured the drinks, and they just sat back quietly and listened to the soft music.

"You know Jordan? I was thinking . . ."

"Yes?"

"As long as tomorrow night is our last night being single, why don't we spend the time moving my things in here?"

"That's a marvelous idea. You won't have need of your hotel room after that, and you can sleep in the guest room if you'd like."

After relaxing for a while, Jordan took Jolene back to the hotel. He had a lot to do to make ready for his new bride.

Chapter 21

Here it was, Friday night already. How much faster the day had gone than was expected. Soon Jordan heard the familiar ring at the front door. Just as he suspected, Jolene was standing there when he opened the door. "I see you're ready to go and pick up your things."

"Yes I am. Do you have any suit

cases that I can use to pack them in?"

"I put them in the car last night when I got home."

"Good, then I guess we might as well get started."

When they reached the Hotel Royale, Jordan went right to Jolene's room with her.

"I hope you don't mind if I help you pack. You can take care of your personal items. I'll help pack your things here in the closet."

Jolene watched how carefully Jordan packed her dresses and coats. She felt proud that she was marrying such a considerate man. The credit for his refinement had to go explicitly to Madame Couquet.

In the train case, she packed her toilet articles and used the over-night bag for her lingerie. It took them almost two hours to finish packing, and now she could say goodbye to this part of her life. With this bright promising future, she felt no remorse. When they got to the desk to check out, the old man seemed surprised to see Jolene leaving so soon.

"Miss Du Bois, I'm sorry to see you leaving."

"We're getting married," she said, as she looked lovingly at Jordan.

"I wish you both happiness. Now, if you'll just wait a moment, I have a refund for you."

"No, please keep it. Maybe someone will come in and need a room and can't pay for it. I will feel contented to know I was able to help someone in distress."

"Okay with me if you're sure of your decision."

"Yes, I am and so long for now."

Jordan was very quiet on the way back to the mansion.

NINE

"What's wrong, hon?"

"Oh, I don't know. I was just thinking about the old superstition of a groom seeing the bride before the marriage."

"That's strange. I was thinking the same thing."

"Well, I've decided to try and avoid you tomorrow."

"That's alright with me. If we open a window again tonight, I'll go out in the morning."

"Fine, but how will you get to the church tomorrow night?

"I've walked the distance before. I can do it again."

"No. Instead of that, I'll call a cab to pick you up here at five after nine tomorrow night. I promise I won't look out until after you've gone."

"Okay if that's the way you want it."

After reaching the mansion, Jordan helped her unpack and put everything in the master bedroom. He showed her to the guest room and made sure everything was to her liking. He waited downstairs until she was settled. When Jolene came down, he fixed her a drink and they sat together in the living room.

"This is really cozy," said Jordan. "I can hardly wait until tomorrow night."

"You've waited this long, so I'm sure 24 hours won't make much difference."

After finishing their drinks, Jolene kissed Jordan and went upstairs to the guest room. Jordan opened the window for her to leave in the morning. He made sure everything was in order, and he too retired.

Chapter 22

When Jordan woke up, he came downstairs quietly. He didn't want to disturb Jolene. He phoned the cab company and requested a cab be sent to the mansion at 9:05pm that night.

After making the call, he went into the den and listened for Jolene. He heard her get up and come downstairs. Right after nine,

Jolene left through the opened window. Jordan came out of the den and waited for the servants to come.

Soon the house was bustling with the familiar chores. Clair was the first to discover Jolene's clothes in the master bedroom. "It looks like the young man has a friend."

Jean said, "Yes, but I'm sure everything is according to Madame Couquet's plan, whatever it is."

"I have a feeling you're right."

"I wonder why they only come here at night."

NINE

"They must really be something to deserve the use of this house."

The servants went about their usual business and before Jordan realized, they were gone again. Jordan went and unlocked the door and returned to the den. Jolene went into the house and quickly dressed. She had decided to wear the white dress and chapel veil she had found amid the wardrobe. Soon she heard a horn blow outside. She ran downstairs and got into the cab. Jordan left the house shortly after he heard the taxi leave.

Jo Ann Zueckert

The lights in the church were on
when he got there. The ceremony
was simple but very beautiful.
When it was over, Jordan took his
new bride back to the mansion.
Since they were in a very romantic
mood, they sat in the living room
and had a few drinks.

Soon they were in the master
bedroom. Jolene changed into
something appropriate and Jordan
was ready and waiting for her.
When they woke up the next morning, the sun was already shining in
the window.

Jolene got up and made breakfast. After they ate, they went upstairs. Jolene made the bed, and they flopped own and fell asleep again.

Millie walked in shortly after and saw the two cats curled up together. "Percy, come quickly!"

Percival, Jean, and Clair all ran when Millie called. They saw Jolene and Jordan on the bed.

Isn't that cute?" said Clair. "I think they've fallen in love."

"It looks like it's too late to break that up," said Percival.

"Well, her choice couldn't have been better," said Millie. "Maybe this is where she's been spending her nights."

Chapter 23

That night, Jordan told Jolene of his plans for a Hawaiian honey-moon. She was naturally all for it. "How will we travel? It won't be easy changing from cats to people and vice versa."

"I have it all figured out. We have a booking for the 9:30pm flight tomorrow night. We'll have enough time to find a place before the change."

"You mean you had it all planned in advance?"

"Yep! We'll have no problems. The night life in Hawaii is supposed to be really swinging. And during the day, we'll just stay in. No one will be the wiser."

"Then we'd better pack."

Jolene got the suitcases out, and they packed enough for a nine-day vacation in the most exquisite place of all. "I wonder what the servants will think when they don't see us for nine days?

"I don't know," said Jordan. "But

this is our life, not theirs."

*　*　*

The next night Jordan drove the Jaguar to the airport in Juneau. It was a 25-minute drive, and they boarded the plane just in time for the take off. Here they were, on their way to the honeymoon that would be anyone's dream come true.

When they finally reached the island, they had just time enough to find a small cabin and settle down for their stay. As they entered the cabin, Jolene laughed. "Look Jordan, number 9. That's the same number as my hotel room in Pilar."

"That's right. I'd almost forgotten about that."

By the time they were completely settled in the cabin, the expected change took place. The two cats spent most of the day exploring their surroundings and taking their usual cat naps.

By nightfall, they were raring to go. The first night they spent sight seeing. They really enjoyed the beautiful view of the famed Diamond Head. Some of the young natives that they met invited them

for a Luau the following night. They
accepted the invitation and returned to the quaint little hut.

While they were enjoying them-
selves, the servants were back
home worrying about the cats.
They couldn't understand why
there had been no sign of them.
They also wondered why the
Jaguar had not retuned as usual.

Percival had decided to keep the
whole thing quiet for at least two
weeks. He'd consoled the women
by reminding them that the car
would be easy to trace since it was
one of a kind. He also showed

them that most of the clothes were still in the house. If those people really weren't' going to return, they would have taken everything with them. They were satisfied with his decision and made up their minds to pretend nothing happened.

Millie faithfully put food out for the cats every day. Much to her surprise, the dishes were always empty in the morning. The servants couldn't understand why the cats would disappear like that, but they kept hoping they would show up soon.

Chapter 24

Jolene and Jordan really enjoyed their stay in Hawaii.

In the nine days they were there, they took in as much night life as possible.

They had tried night surfing and swimming. They'd gone to Luaus and had seen the native Hula and flaming sword dancers. They had done so much in those nine nights that they were almost glad to be returning home. When they reached the airport in Juneau, they got into the jaguar and headed straight to the mansion. Jolene decided to unpack the suitcases in the morning.

When morning came, they only heard the familiar voices of the servants. They had overslept, and now it was too late to worry about unpacking. Millie was happy to see that the cats were back home. "It's a funny thing, but they came home and now the car is here again."

"Yes," said Percival. "Maybe

whoever it is that takes the car borrowed the cats for a while."

"I wonder why," said Jean.

"Well, maybe they had some children to visit and wanted them to see the cats."

"That's possible," said Jean, quite satisfied with Percy's conclusion.

*   *   *

The next two months went by quickly. Everyone noticed how fat Jolene was getting. Percival joked with Millie and told her he thought she was going to become a grandmother soon. Not long after that,

Jo Ann Zueckert

Clair came running into the
kitchen. "Come quickly everyone.
Jolene is up in the master bedroom
and she just had a baby kitten!"

By the time they all got there,
two little kittens had been born.
Before long, a third one came
along. There was the proud father
sitting next to her, looking on.

"Isn't this wonderful? Three
beautiful baby kittens!" said Jean.
In their excitement, they hadn't
heard the doorbell. Percival finally
answered the door after the third
ring. It was Mr. Anderson, the
lawyer, with a big envelope.

NINE

"I'm sorry to disturb you but I have this letter which was supposed to be delivered today. Madame Couquet wrote this letter before she died and asked me to personally deliver it on this day."

"Thank you very much," said Percival as he said goodbye to Mr. Anderson.

"Let's all go to the living room. I'll read this letter aloud. It really looks important."

After they were all seated, Percival began to read:

Jo Ann Zueckert

To my Dear, Loyal Servants,

As you well know, I have asked
you to refrain from entering
the mansion every night from
9:00pm until 9:00am the fol-
lowing morning. I know this
was a strange request, but
tonight you will understand
why. On this, the ninth day of
the ninth month, I want you to
return to the house at 9:05pm.
Upon entering, you will under-
stand why I wanted you to
honor my wishes.

Good luck to all of you,

Madame Francene Couquet

"Wow, its weird receiving a letter from someone who is already dead."

"That's right, Jean. I wonder what's in store for us?" asked Millie.

"We'll all know tonight. Now, let's go and check on our new little family." Percival said this as he started out of the room.

When they got upstairs, the exhausted Jolene was lying there nursing her kittens. This was certainly a sight to see. One big happy family!

Jo Ann Zueckert

Chapter 25

The servants left the mansion as they had done previously. They had no idea what to expect when they returned at 9:05pm.

When the time did come, Percival stood in front of the women and rang the bell. There were lights on in the mansion, and they could hear voices. Jordan answered the door."Well, hello!

Jo Ann Zueckert

Percival, come right in"

As the servants walked into the
vestibule, they could not understand how this handsome stranger
knew them. When they entered the
living room, Jolene was seated on
one end of the couch, and three
little bundles were wrapped up
next to her.

Jolene jumped up and hugged
Percival and Millie. Millie's mind
could still not grasp this situation.
Percy spoke first. "Who are you?
How do you know us?"

Jordan's reply answered both
questions at once. "I am Jordan,

and this is Jolene."

Clair was so put aback on this statement. All she could say was, "You mean the cats??!!"

"That's right! Madame Couquet put some sort of spell on us that changed us from cats to people and vice versa."

"You mean, all this time, it was you who took the car?" asked Jean.

"Yes. I don't know what purpose we have served. All I know is this is all part of some plan."

Millie spoke up, "Then I guess that these babies are sort of . . . sort of like . . . my grandchildren!"

"If you want them to be, then they truly are," said Jolene.

The servants found it very hard to believe, but after talking to Jordan and Jolene for a while, they were certain that their incredible story had to be true. Millie, Jean, and Clair each took one of the babies. As they went upstairs with Jolene, Percival began talking to Jordan.

"I just don't know what to make of all this. How is it possible?"

"Madame Couquet was one of the few who possessed such power. It was lucky she was a good woman. If she had been the slightest bit evil, no telling what she could have done."

"In all the years that we worked for her, I could never honestly say she used her powers."

"No, I guess only to slight degrees."

"Yes, I do remember a few incidents that were unexplainable at the time."

"This spell that she put on Jolene and me must have been the greatest achievement of all time."

"All I can say is its marvelous! Millie and I always wanted a child, but were never blessed with one. We had always considered Jolene our baby."

"So far as I am concerned, she is as much your daughter as I am Madame Couquet's son. She too, always wanted a child and treated me like a son. Since I have inherited the entire estate, I feel that I am her son!"

"Then would you mind if Millie and I consider ourselves grandparents?"

"It would be an honor."

Chapter 26

The women were all upstairs.
Each one took charge of changing
a baby. Jean and Claire took the
boys, and Millie took the girl.
Jolene now could relax for a while.
Jean asked her what she had
named the babies.

"First born is Alan Otis, second is
Brian Thomas, and the girl is
Charlene Theresa."

"Beautiful names for darling babies," Jean commented.

"Thank you."

"Tomorrow we'll have to go out and get some baby furniture for the little angels."

"Yes, and we'll need complete layettes for them too," said Clair.

In the morning, the servants returned to the mansion expecting go see the family of cats.

Much to their surprise, Jordan and Jolene had not changed! Upon entering the house last night, the spell had been broken. This then, began the new life for the

Couquets. Even though Millie and Percival were now adopted grandparents, they insisted on continuing their services as they had in the past.

*   *   *

Three years went by, and Jolene presented her family with a new set of triplets. This time a boy and two girls, Duncan Francis, Eilene Fredrica, and Francene Serena. Having triplets twice had not proved a difficult task for Jolene. She had all the help she needed. Jean, Clair, and Millie took over whenever she asked. She enjoyed her children and was able to spend enough time with each one to make them feel like individuals. At times, she wished Madame Couquet could be here to see them. She somehow felt that wherever she was, she was looking down on them proudly.

Life was far from difficult for the Couquet family but Jordan insisted on bringing up his children properly. Even though they could afford everything, the children did not get all they asked for. Jordan wanted them to grow up to be upstanding citizens. He could be proud of their

behavior no matter where they
went.

*   *   *

Here it was, nine years since the
magic spell. Jolene was rushing
around, getting the six older children ready for their first day of
school. Alan, Brian, and Charlene
were entering the fourth grade.
Duncan, Eilene, and Francene
would be starting kindergarten.
The three-year-old triplets, Gorden
Silas, Helene Eliza, and Irene
Norma were excited about seeing
their older brothers and sisters off
to school. The big family walked

down the winding driveway to await the school bus.

As the big yellow-orange bus rounded the bend, Jolene noticed the large black number 9 painted on the side.

"That's strange," she said to Jordan, "This is September 9th, school bus number 9, we have 9 children, our whole lives seem to center on that number."

"I guess that is indeed our lucky number!"

When they returned to the house, Clair seemed very excited.

"What is it Clair?"

NINE

"Look! I was just writing the children's names and discovered something. All the girls' first names rhyme with Jolene, and the boys' names rhyme with Jordan."

Jolene looked, "You're right! I didn't even plan it that way."

"Not only that, but their first names begin with the first nine letters of the alphabet."

Jordan looked at the paper. "Did you also notice that the girls' middle names all rhyme, and the boys' too?"

"Yes, and if you notice, the middle names begin with the same letters, as the numbers one through nine!"

"This must have been destined," said Jolene. "The names just seemed to pop into my head like magic."

"Yes," said Jordan, "our magic family of nine!"

www.ingramcontent.com/pod-product-compliance
Lightning Source LLC
Chambersburg PA
CBHW050932120626
46552CB00001B/174